MAY 26 '75

JUL 8 '75

STO

ALLEN COUNTY PUBLIC LIBRARY

**FRIENDS
OF ACPL**

P9-BTY-185

THE THIRD GIFT

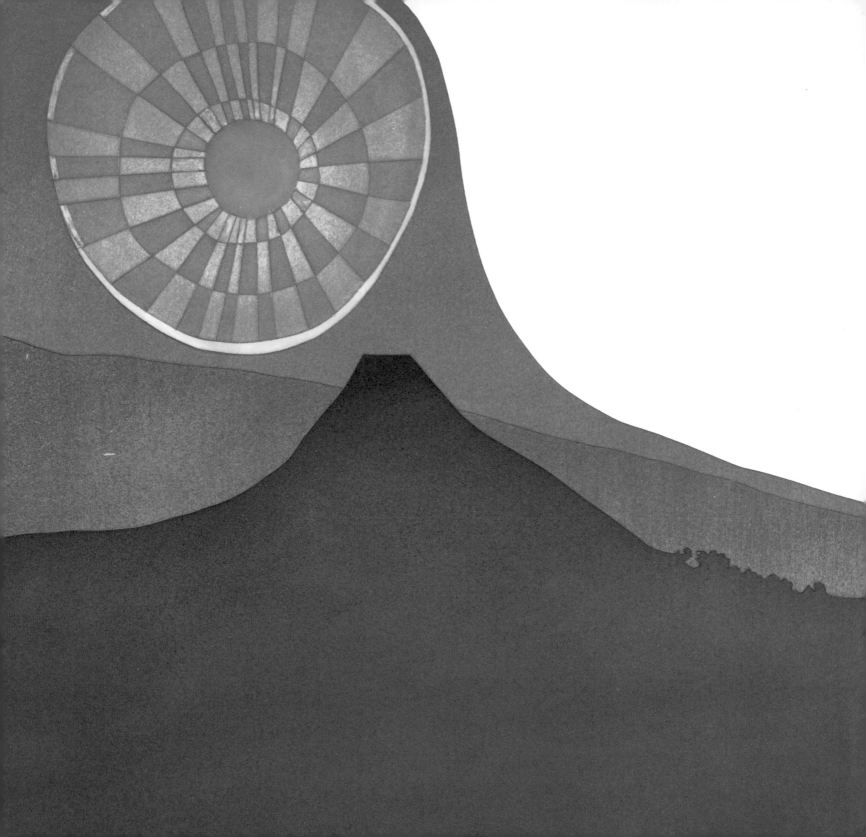

THE THIRD GIFT

by **Jan Carew**
Illustrated by **Leo and Diane Dillon**

Little, Brown and Company
BOSTON   TORONTO

ILLUSTRATIONS COPYRIGHT © 1974 BY LEO AND DIANE DILLON

TEXT COPYRIGHT © 1974 BY JAN CAREW

ALL RIGHTS RESERVED. NO PART OF THIS BOOK MAY BE REPRO-
DUCED IN ANY FORM OR BY ANY ELECTRONIC OR MECHANICAL
MEANS INCLUDING INFORMATION STORAGE AND RETRIEVAL
SYSTEMS WITHOUT PERMISSION IN WRITING FROM THE PUB-
LISHER, EXCEPT BY A REVIEWER. WHO MAY QUOTE BRIEF PAS-
SAGES IN A REVIEW.

FIRST EDITION

T 06/74

Library of Congress Cataloging in Publication Data

Carew, Jan.
    The third gift.

    [1. Africa--Fiction] I. Dillon, Leo, illus.
II. Dillion, Diane, illus. III. Title.
PZ7.C2119Th   [Fic]   73-12061
ISBN 0-316-12847-3

Published simultaneously in Canada
by Little, Brown & Company (Canada) Limited

PRINTED IN THE UNITED STATES OF AMERICA

U. S. 1822697

THE THIRD GIFT

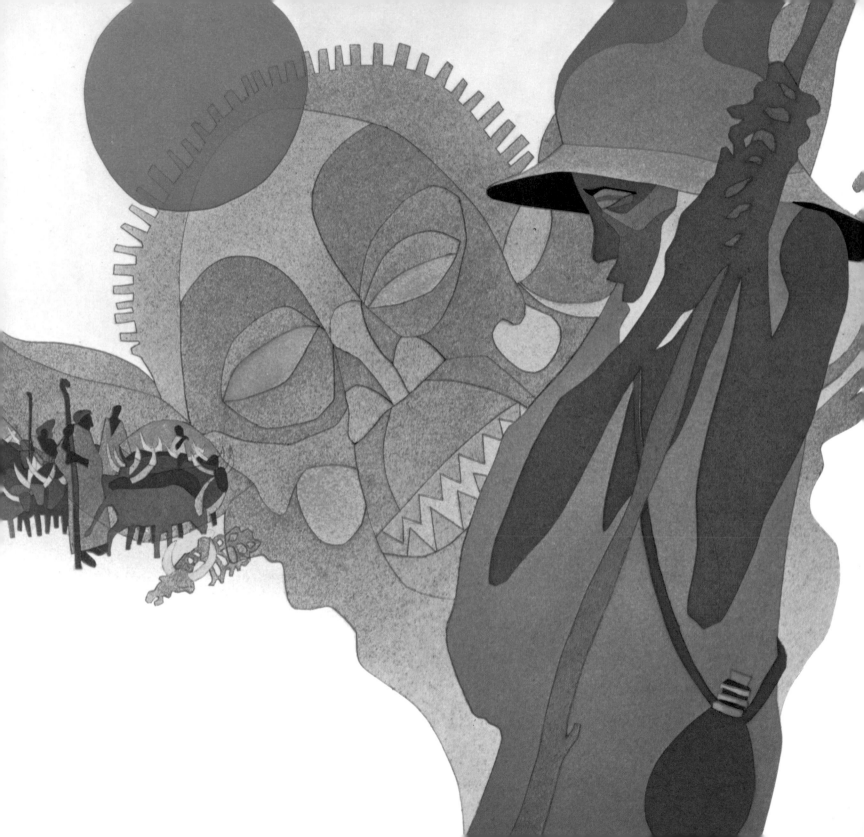

In long-time-past days there was a black prophet named Amakosa who was the leader of the Jubas—a clan of herdsmen and wanderers. When Amakosa felt age nesting inside his tired limbs, and was certain that the soft footsteps he heard following him were those of Mantop, Death's messenger boy, he summoned the elders of the clan to a palaver. It was a time when endless seasons of drought and dust were scattering the Jubas and their herds like silk cotton blossoms in the wind, and the clan was threatened with extinction.

The elders gathered in a circle and drank libations. As the sacred gourd was passed around, dark hands, lean and veined, trembled like leaves.

Amakosa, with his old and cunning eyes gleaming in nests of wrinkled flesh, said calmly, "We must find green pastures, and places where the wind brings rain, and where the vampire sun is no longer king."

"Ai! Ai!," the people said in a chorus, "lead us there and we will follow you."

So the Jubas picked up their belongings and followed Amakosa across the parched savannahs where the wind had bent the thorn trees like old men's backs and where the stunted elephant grass hissed like snakes. Through endless seasons of waxing and waning moons, they left a trail of bones picked clean by vultures and bleached by the sun. One evening, when the gloaming was giving way to starlight and pale lightnings, they came to the foot of a mountain whose peak was lost in the stars. They washed their dirty limbs in cool streams and threw themselves down on the innocent grass, wherever sleep surprised them.

They woke up at day—clean refreshed, and stretching themselves like ocelots, they asked, "What is this mountain called, Amakosa?"

"It has no name, so we will call it Nameless Mountain," Amakosa said.

"And what is this place called, Amakosa?"

"We will call it Arisa, the place of springs."

The Jubas settled in Arisa, and when Mantop, Death's messenger boy, finally knocked on his door, Amakosa called all the Jubas together and said,

"Listen well to what I have to say. My face has beaten against many years, and now Mantop has sent for me. You must choose a leader to succeed me. When I have gone, all the young men must make their way up Nameless Mountain. The one that climbs the highest and brings back a gift of the wonders that he saw, him you must make your leader."

The Jubas were silent when Mantop led their prophet
away. When sunset was casting long shadows, they saw
the two—a headless man with a flute stuck in his throat

and the old man Amakosa, bent with the weight of his years—walking towards the River of Night. And at day-clean even the wind was heavy with lamentation.

Then all the young men set out up Nameless Mountain—up past the orchids and wild vines on the mossy face of the rocks, up to where the wild mango stripes the slopes with white blossoms, up to where secret springs gurgle into rivers. Up and up they climbed until all they could hear was the wind in the stranger-trees and the echoes of drums on the plains. Towards evening one man came back weary and sleepy as mud, and the others followed dragging their feet. But the one that climbed the highest came running deer-speed down the mountainside holding something in his hand high above his head. He didn't stop until he reached the village square. The Jubas crowded around him and chorused, "Show us the wonderful thing you brought, Brother-Man!"

And the young man said, "Come closer and see." He opened his hand and declared, "This is what I have brought. Eye never saw and hand never touched a gift like this."

And the women cried out with wonder, "Look at the curve of it and the way it catches the light! It is truly a wondrous thing!"

The gift that the young man brought was a stone, and when this stone caught the light, it had all the colors of mountain orchids and rainbows and more.

"But what is the message in this stone?" the people asked.

"This stone brings us the gift of Work," the young man said. "Since we wandered into this green country we have become idle, and idleness is a more terrible threat than drought or hunger."

And looking at the stone all of the Jubas had a vision of ploughshares and axe blades, endless fields of maize and cassava, and harvest times filled with the songless singing of their drums.

Jawa, the man who had brought the gift of Work, ruled for a long time. The Juba nation multiplied, and the memory of hunger and laziness was pushed far away from them.

But the time came when Mantop, Death's messenger boy, knocked on Jawa's door of reeds, and he, too, had to walk the trail to the River of Night. The lamentation weighed heavy on the hearts of those he left behind.

So, once again at fore-day-morning, the young men set out up Nameless Mountain. And Kabo, the man who climbed the highest this time, came down the mountainside soft-softly. He could not hurry because the gift he brought was a mountain flower. When he stood in the center of the village square holding this marvelous Flower in his hand, it was clear for all to see that he had brought his people the gift of Beauty. They crowded around him to marvel at the curve of the petals and the colors and the way the pistil caught the light and made the pollen glitter like jewels. The singing drums and the song-makers sang Kabo's praises far into the night.

Kabo ruled through many moons, and the Juba country became a place to wonder at. The door of every house had flowers painted on it in bright vermilion colors; the girls wore flowers in their hair; flowers without number were carved out of wood and stone, and every canoe was built with a flower sculpted on its prow.

But, the Jubas grew dissatisfied. They had Work and Beauty and yet they wanted more. Some began to mutter that they were thinking of moving to another country down the river and across the plains. So when Mantop sent for Kabo everyone knew that his successor would have to bring back a powerful gift from Nameless Mountain to hold the nation together.

Kabo went on his journey to the River of Night quietly, and for the third time the young men set out up Nameless Mountain. Amongst them was a dreaming, sad-faced son of Tiho the Hunter who was called Ika, the Quiet One. Ika always looked as if he was gnawing at the bones of everlasting griefs.

He took a trail on the far side of Nameless Mountain where none of the others dared follow. When night fell and the fireflies brightened the fields and forests like fallen stars, everyone returned except Ika.

And the weary ones who had returned said, "We saw him parting the clouds and climbing up and up, and none of us had the strength to follow him."

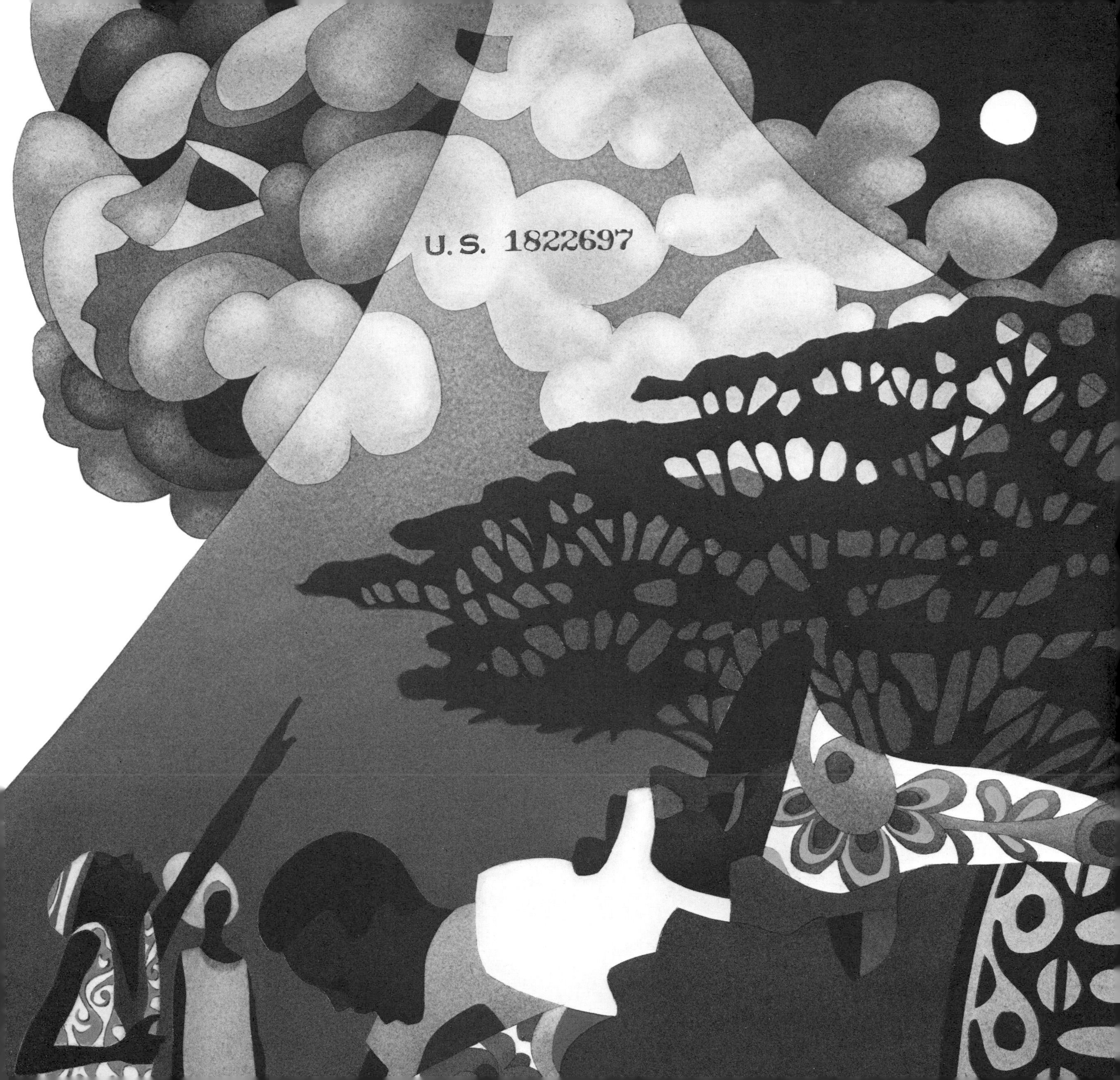
U.S. 1822697

When Ika did not return by the next morning, the Jubas sent search parties to look for him and posted lookouts on the mountainside. Sun and Moon lengthened many shadows; still Ika did not return. There was plenty of talk about him and how he had gone his lonesome way to die on Nameless Mountain.

But one morning bright with dew and singing birds, Ika came running down the mountainside, parting the long grass and leaping from rock to rock. He was clenching his fist and holding his hand high above his head. He reached the river bank and crossed the cassava fields, trampling down the young plants. When he came to the village square he did not stop.

And the people said, "Aye, aye, Ika, you're home, man! We were waiting for you until our hearts were becoming weary with waiting."

But he kept on running, and again they shouted, "You're home, man! Ika, you're home!"

Ika would have run right across the village square and away towards the fields of elephant grass if he had not tripped on a piece of firewood. He fell and lay panting as though his chest was going to burst, still keeping his fist clenched.

"What gift have you brought us, Brother-Man? Talk to us. What did you see above the clouds on Nameless Mountain?"

For a long time Ika could find no words to answer them. But Leza, the Healer, came and anointed him with kuru oil. The men could not wait to see the gift he had brought; so they pried his fist open. But when they opened Ika's hand, it was empty.

When Ika found his tongue again, he said, "I went up to the clouds and over and above them, and I don't know how long it took because past the clouds was a brightness that blinded my eyes. Then there came a time when all I felt was a soft carpet under my feet, and when I breathed in the mountain air, it was like drawing knife blades up my nostrils. When my sight came back I found myself on the mountain top. . . ."

"Lord! You must've seen the whole world from there, Ika!" a young man exclaimed.

"Yes, and while I stood up there a soft white thing like rain started to fall . . . and yet it wasn't rain because it fell like leaves when there is no wind. I gathered this downy whiteness in my hand, but the farther down the mountainside I ran, the less of it I was holding, so I went back for more and ran down the mountain again. Four times I did this, and every time I was heading for home bird-speed, this magic thing melted in my hand. All I bring with me now is the memory of it, the feel of the sky and the bite of the wind—and the fire and ice burning my hand."

And the people listening believed, for this quiet young man, when he did speak, could warble like singing-birds-sweet, and when he spoke, his words would grow inside your head like seeds.

Ika became prophet of the Jubas for he had brought the best gift of all, the gift of Fantasy, of Imagination and of Faith. So, with the gifts of Work and Beauty and Imagination, the Jubas became poets and bards and creators, and they live at the foot of Nameless Mountain to this day.